Grandfather's Rock

An Italian Folktale

JOEL STRANGIS

Illustrated by RUTH GAMPER

Houghton Mifflin Company

Boston 1993

For my Grandmothers, Rubelle and Dorothy—J.S.

For Mutti and Wilhelm—R.G.

Library of Congress Cataloging-in-Publication Data

Strangis, Joel.
  Grandfather's rock / Joel Strangis ; illustrated by Ruth Gamper.
    p. cm.
  Summary: A poor family in Italy finds a way to keep their elderly
Grandfather with them instead of sending him to live in a home for
old people.
  ISBN 0-395-65367-3
  [1. Grandfathers—Fiction. 2. Old age—Fiction. 3. Italy—
Fiction.]   I. Gamper, Ruth, ill. II. Title.
PZ7.S8978Gr 1993   92-26525
[E]—dc20   CIP
                AC

Printed in the United States of America

WOZ 10 9 8 7 6 5 4 3 2 1

IN THE OLD DAYS, a family lived in the south of Italy. There was a father, a mother, a son named Marco, and three daughters: Prima, who was the oldest; Aldora, who was the tallest; and Paula, who was the youngest. They had a small farm with a beautiful view of the sea below and the mountains above. The land was steep and rocky though, and no matter how hard Mother and Father worked, the family remained poor.

One day Father came home from visiting Grandfather. He told his family, "Grandfather is old. He cannot live by himself anymore. Tomorrow we must bring him to live with us."

The children loved Grandfather and were happy he was coming to live with them. Mother, however, was very practical, and she worried about one more person in the family.

"I love Grandfather too, but we cannot feed ourselves. How will we feed him?" she asked.

"He fed me before I could work," answered Father. "Now that he cannot work, I will feed him."

The next morning Father, Marco, Prima, Aldora, and Paula
went down the hill to get Grandfather. Returning home, Father
carried Grandfather on his back. Walking behind Father were

Prima and Aldora carrying Grandfather's bed and Marco carrying his chair. Last in line was Paula, carrying Grandfather's pillow and taking very big steps with her very small legs.

That night Mother made supper with all the food they had—a loaf of bread, five eggs, and a pitcher of milk. During supper, everyone listened as Grandfather told of his adventures on the sea. He told a story of strange people and beautiful palaces far away. At the end of the story, Prima said she wanted to be a great sailor and travel across the sea. Paula said she wanted to be a princess and live in a palace.

The next day, after Father had left for the fields, the children took Grandfather to the ruins of an ancient temple. There he told them stories of great battles to defend the temple against raiders from the sea. Marco dreamed of being a fierce raider, while Aldora imagined herself bravely defending the temple.

The children had a wonderful day, but Mother was unhappy. When Father came home from the fields she told him, "The children will not work. All they do is listen to Grandfather's stories. No one has collected the eggs. No one has milked the cow."

"Grandfather told me stories when I was young," said Father. "Now he must tell his grandchildren stories. I will collect the eggs. I will milk the cow."

A few days later Mother said, "Our wood pile is almost gone. Grandfather needs a fire at night, but Grandfather does not cut wood."

"Grandfather is too old to cut wood," said Father. "He kept me warm when I was young. I will cut wood now."

Finally one evening Mother told Father, "Winter is coming. We do not have enough food or wood. If Grandfather stays with us, we will all starve. You did not stay in his house forever. He cannot stay in your house forever. You must take him to the home for old

people, in the village on the other side of the hill."

Father was awake all night thinking about his family. He loved them all. He wanted to take care of Grandfather, but he also had to take care of his wife, his son, and his daughters.

Early the next morning, Father announced that Grandfather
would have to live in the home for old people. Grandfather nodded
his head. The girls hugged Grandfather. Marco noticed a tear on
his mother's cheek.

Father loaded Grandfather on his back and started up the road

to the village on the other side of the hill. Walking behind Father
were Prima and Aldora carrying Grandfather's bed and Marco
carrying his chair. Far behind, walking slowly with very small
steps, was Paula carrying Grandfather's pillow.

On the way up the hill, they saw a single olive tree with
twisted branches. The lonely tree was even older than Grandfather.
As they passed the tree, everyone made promises to Grandfather.

"I will visit you every Sunday," said Father.

"I will never forget your birthday," said Marco.

"We will write you every week," said Prima and Aldora.

"I will send you chocolates at Christmas," called Paula from the rear.

When they had left the olive tree behind, the children whispered among themselves. "We must keep Grandfather with us," said Marco.

"Prima, you are the oldest," said Aldora. "You must find a way so that we can keep Grandfather."

"What did she say?" called Father.

Marco answered in a loud voice, "Aldora says she's tired
and she wishes we had some water."

"At the top of this hill," said Father, "in the grove of trees,
is a large rock. We can rest there."

Father reached the rock first. It was a beautiful rock, shaded by tall trees. He placed Grandfather on the rock and dipped water from the nearby stream.

Prima, Aldora, and Marco put down the bed and the chair and climbed up on the rock. Prima sat in the middle, her brother and

sister on one side, her father and her grandfather on the other.
Paula was still coming up the hill.

Prima's stomach hurt. She knew the next stop would be the
home for old people. She knew she had to do something, now.

Prima took a deep breath. "Father," she said, "thank you for showing us this rock."

"You're welcome," said Father.

"This is an excellent place to rest. We will call this 'Grandfather's Rock,'" continued Prima. "And we will rest on Grandfather's Rock, Father, when we carry you to the home for old people."

Marco winked at Aldora.

Father looked at his children. He looked at Grandfather. He placed his hand on Grandfather's Rock.

Then Father picked up Grandfather, turned around, and started for the path leading back down the hill.

"Hurrah!" shouted Aldora and Marco as they jumped off the rock. "We're all going home!"

"Hurrah!" shouted Paula, who had just reached the clearing and now immediately turned for home.

"But what will we tell Mother?" asked Father as he waited for the older children to pick up Grandfather's belongings. "How will we feed Grandfather? How will we feed ourselves?"

"I will milk the cow and Aldora will collect the eggs," said Prima. "So you can spend more time in the fields, and raise more crops."

"I will cut wood for our fire," offered Marco. "I will cut enough wood to sell to our neighbors, too."

Hearing his children speak, Father carried Grandfather just
a little bit higher as they went down the hill. Walking behind
Father were Prima and Aldora carrying Grandfather's bed and

Marco carrying his chair. And way ahead, running as fast as
her legs would move, was Paula carrying Grandfather's pillow.
Grandfather, by the way, was carrying a very big smile.